USBORNE HOTSHOTS

SPYING
FOR BEGINNERS

USBORNE HOTSHOTS

SPYING
FOR BEGINNERS

Edited by Lisa Miles
Designed by Karen Tomlins

Illustrated by Colin King

Series editor: Judy Tatchell
Series designer: Ruth Russell

Based on material by
Falcon Travis, Judy Hindley,
Ruth Thompson, Heather Amery,
Christopher Rawson and
Anita Harper

CONTENTS

About spying

Real spies work for governments and big corporations. They work in secret, finding out information about new weapons or new inventions, for instance. Spies use false identities and cunning methods of passing on secret information.

This book is based on the techniques that real spies use. Read on and find out how to be a master spy!

Secret messages

Spies pass messages to other spies in their group, who are known as contacts. To prevent your messages falling into enemy hands, always exchange information secretly.

You can exchange information by leaving messages in hiding places and by writing them in code. Always remember – the enemy may be watching your every move.

Following people

Spies may need to follow people without being seen. Good spies can follow people through both the town and countryside. You may have to change your tactics depending on the route the person takes.

4

Disguises

Spies wear disguises so that they won't be recognized by enemy spies. A good disguise will help you watch someone without being noticed. If they begin to suspect you, you can change your disguise quickly to keep them guessing.

False identity

When spies go out to do their secret work, they give themselves a new identity – a false name and address. For your new identity, you could even pretend to come from a foreign country. Here's how.

Diary with false names and places

Money from foreign country

Write letters to yourself, using your false name.

False family photograph

Real spies take out clothes-labels that might show where they really come from.

Foreign newspaper cutting

Foreign bus and rail tickets

Foreign stamps

When pretending to be foreign, your money, photos and letters must come from your pretend country. Save foreign stamps, coins and tickets from trips to other countries. Cut out pictures from magazines to use as "photos" of your home. Real spies check that their clothing and luggage will not give them away.

Secret messages

Good spies exchange messages so secretly that enemy spies never see them do it. Here are some tips on how to swap secrets.

Carrying messages

Don't attract your enemy's attention by carrying suspicious-looking papers. Instead, use tiny pieces of paper and hide them in the places shown in the picture.

Remove the message with a quick, casual movement. Don't look anxious.

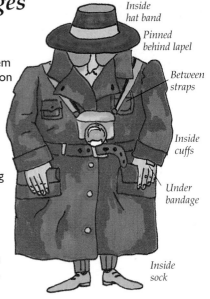

Inside hat band

Pinned behind lapel

Between straps

Inside cuffs

Under bandage

Inside sock

The rendezvous

A *rendezvous* is a place where spies and their contacts arrange to meet each other. This art gallery on the right is a *rendezvous*.

psst – plan x!

The spies pretend to look at the paintings – hoping to put their enemy off the scent.

The spy on the right drops her guidebook as if by accident. It holds a message!

Her contact picks it up, but quickly swaps it for his own. He keeps hers.

6

Mailbox method

This spy never meets his contact, but often goes to the library that his contact uses.

The librarian passes the spy's message to his contact for him. She is called a "mailbox".

Using a drop

This spy never meets his contact, but leaves him messages at an agreed spot.

In spy language this is called a "drop". Later, the contact visits the drop and collects messages.

Signposts

You need several drops in case one is spotted by the enemy. You also need another agreed hiding place, called a signpost.

You can leave a sign at the signpost to show your contact which drop you have used. A chalk mark might do the trick.

Drop 1

Drop 2

Drop 3

Signpost with secret mark

Quick codes

Spies need to write their messages in code, just in case they fall into enemy hands. Messages that are not in code are called "plain" messages.

Here are some codes to make your messages secret. Each code scrambles the letters in a different way. The names of the codes give a hint to how they work. Here's how to code the message "TRICK THE ENEMY".

Rev-Random

1. Write the message back to front.
2. Break it into new groups.

YMENE EHT KCIRT

YMEN EEHTK CIRT

Bi-Rev

1. Pair up the letters.
2. Write each pair backward.

TR IC KT HE EN EMY

RT CI TK EH NE YME

Rev-Groups

1. Group the message-letters differently.
2. Write each group backward.

TRI CKT HEENE MY

IRT TKC ENEEH YM

Mid-Null

1. Break the message into even-numbered groups of letters.
2. Split each group into halves.
3. Put a dummy letter (a null) between the halves in each group.

TRIC KTHE ENEM Y

TR IC KT HE EN EM Y

TRMIC KTLHE ENOEM Y

Sandwich

1. Write out half of the message, leaving spaces between letters.
2. Write the second half in the spaces.
3. Then group the letters differently.

T R I C K T H

TE RE IN CE KM TY H

TER EIN CEKM TYH

8

Hiding a message

Spies are always on the lookout for places to hide their coded messages. Here are some.

1. Behind a notice.
2. Between cracks in stone.
3. Under a loose paving slab.
4. Stuck under a bench.
5. Under lifted turf.

How to break the code

Write the message letters from the end and see if they begin to form into words.

Reverse the first few pairs of letters and see if you can join them into words.

Reverse the letters in each group and look for words.

Cross out the middle letter in each group. Try joining the rest of the letters into words.

Starting with the first letter, write down every other letter. Then write down the letters that were in between them.

Alphabet code

Make up a code which substitutes one letter for another. For instance, A might be coded as L, B as M, C as N, and so on through the alphabet. In this code, CAB would be coded as NLM.

To decode the message, see if any letters appear frequently. If so, these might be the common vowels A, E, I or O. Most words have at least one. Then note patterns of paired letters. Common pairs are TT, LL and SS. Some letters, such as A, I, H, W and U are very rarely paired.

As you guess the meaning of each code letter, write it down beneath each example of that letter throughout the message. The real message will soon take shape.

Check your security

A successful spy ring (group of spies) must have good security. That is, it must be sure that no enemy spies are finding out its secrets. Here's how to find out if your secrets are safe.

Paper or thread test

Fold up a message, ready for hiding. Open it out and put two tiny pieces of white paper or thread in the first crease.

Put paper in the second crease too. Hide the message and check it later. If the pieces are gone, the message has been opened.

Jam test

Write a message and fold it in half. Smear jam very thinly on the back of the paper.

Any fingerprints will show up on the jam. Do not touch it with your own fingers.

Tricking the enemy...

If your enemy is discovering your secrets, here's how to stop him. First choose a false drop.

Then attract attention by looking as suspicious as you can. Get the suspect to follow you.

Once you are being followed, lead the enemy to the false drop in a winding, roundabout way.

Watching and being watched

Try not to look directly at a suspect unless you are sure that he is not looking at you or that he cannot see you.

Pretend that you are not interested in him. Better still, pretend that you have not even noticed that he is there at all.

An enemy may watch you only because he has seen you watching him. If so, get out of sight and show no interest.

To scare off an enemy, you could try staring at him. He will probably disappear quickly and you can continue with your job.

...and losing him

Go to the drop but do not let the enemy see if you are delivering or collecting a message.

Later, the enemy will check the drop. As it is empty, he will think you were collecting a message.

The enemy has now given himself away. He will watch the false drop and you can just disappear.

Secret writing

You can hide a secret message by writing with invisible ink. You could write a dummy letter to a member of your spy ring, but write the true message in invisible ink in case the letter falls into enemy hands.

Spit method

Sharpen the end of a matchstick. Wet the end with spit and write lightly. Hold the paper to the light to check the writing.

To see the spit message, brush the paper with watery ink. The message shows up darker.

Juice method

Use a matchstick as before. Poke the fleshy part of an apple with the matchstick to collect juice. Write with it.

Cooked juice turns brown.

To see the juice message, heat in a cool oven (about 250°F, 120°C, Gas Mark 2).

Wax method

Chip off some drips from a used, unlit candle. With warm hands, roll the pieces into a pen shape. Then write with it.

Chalk sticks to wax.

To see the wax message, sprinkle the paper with chalk dust. Then shake it off.

Secret maps

As well as secret writing, you can use the methods above to draw spy maps with details of your drops, *rendezvous* and headquarters.

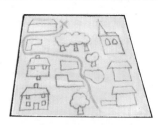

12

Secret indicators

Letters to members of your spy ring should contain clues, or indicators, to tell them what method you have used for your invisible writing. A good system might be, when you date the letter, to use days of the week to mean different writing methods. Use times of day to mean different places on the paper where the message is hidden.

On this letter, "Thursday" means that this is a wax message. "1pm" means that the invisible writing is written down the sides of the paper.

Use a false initial to show that there is an invisible message inside. The spy's real middle name is Edward!

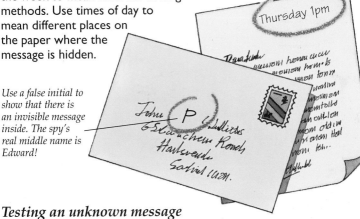

Testing an unknown message

1. Use chalk to test for wax.
2. Use heat to test for juice.
3. Use a wash (watery ink) to test for spit message.

If your contact has forgotten to include an indicator or if you have intercepted a message from an enemy spy, here's what to do.

First look for tell-tale glints by holding the paper at an angle to the light. Any glints might show where the secret writing might be.

Then do the tests in the order shown on the chart.

Stalking

A good spy can follow someone, known as their quarry, without being noticed. In the countryside, you have to move quietly and stay hidden. This is called stalking. If you lose sight of your quarry, look for clues to keep on the trail. This is called tracking.

How to stalk

When stalking a quarry, your clothes should blend into your surroundings. Mixtures of browns and greens are the best to wear. Remember that the crack of a breaking twig or a flicker of movement may give you away.

Stalking walks and crawls

When you are stalking an enemy spy, make use of things that can hide you, like walls and bushes. These are called cover.

In good cover (in trees for example) you can walk upright. Keep your arms still and your hands by your sides.

Near low cover, crouch to keep your head down. Hold your thighs to keep in position. Lift your feet, don't drag them.

Try crawling on your hands and knees, keeping your back low. Lift your hands and knees. This is called the feline crawl.

This is the seal crawl. Lie flat with your legs together and toes turned out. Pull with your arms and push with your toes.

14

Using cover

The spy in the black hat will easily be seen. The spy in the brown hat is making good use of the shape of the tree trunk.

When peering around a wall or tree, one eye is enough. This hides the shape of your head. Keep your head still.

How to track

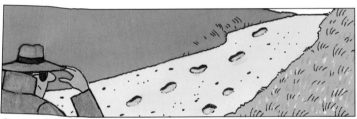

Careless spies might leave tracks behind them to show where they have gone. Look out for footprints.

When searching the ground, shield your eyes and look in the direction of the sun. Small dents in the earth will show up more.

Covering your tracks

Don't be a careless spy. When you are in the countryside, follow these tips to prevent someone tracking you.

Walk on the hardest part of the path. If you have to walk on mud, you could walk backward to leave a false trail.

Don't leave wet footprints. Use stepping stones to cross streams. Step on big leaves to avoid making footprints in sand.

Shadowing

A good spy needs to be able to follow a quarry through towns. You have to follow your quarry at all times without appearing to be watching. This is called shadowing.

How to shadow

You must be able to merge into the background so that your quarry never notices you. Follow closely enough so that you don't lose contact, but not so closely that you look suspicious.

Window check

If you can see your quarry's reflection, it means that he can see yours.

To see if he is watching you, move so he cannot see your reflection.

If he is watching you, he will move to try to catch sight of you again.

Shadow's kit

Using your eyes

To help you shadow your quarry, it might be useful to carry a quick disguise, like a hat and a scarf.

If your quarry sees you, make a quick change in a doorway. You can then continue shadowing.

Good spies learn how to use their eyes without moving their heads – like in this picture.

Corners

Keep a sharp lookout when your quarry gets close to a corner.

If you are not looking, he may be out of sight before you realize.

Hurry after him, but slow down before you reach the corner.

Saunter around casually, so that you don't give yourself away.

Double-mirror trick

Use this double mirror to spy over your shoulder. Here's how to make one.

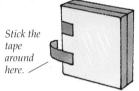

Stick the tape around here.

Tape two pocket mirrors together on one side, so that they can be opened.

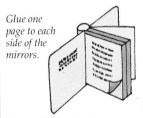

Glue one page to each side of the mirrors.

Tear all but the first and last pages from an old diary. Slip the mirrors between them.

Alternatively, you can just slip the mirrors inside a book or comic.

Shaking off a tail

Remember that enemy spies might try to shadow you too. Try to think about what they might do and how you can avoid being followed or "tailed".

Use tricks to get away from the enemy.

How to shake off a tail

To make sure that you are not followed, plan your route carefully. Don't approach your destination by a direct route. Use a zig-zag or roundabout path. Vary your route so that you don't go the same way every time. Stroll rather than walk fast.

If you decide that you are being followed, here are some ways to try to shake off your tail.

Use the reflections in windows to check whether you've got a tail.

To cross the street, wait until you can be shielded from view by someone.

Dodge up a side street when your tail's view is blocked.

Turn-about trick

Stop in the street and pause. Often your tail will stop too. Turn and walk in his direction.

If your tail walks away, you can disappear down a side street while his back is turned.

18

Bedtime decoy

Real spies do secret work at night. They might leave dummies behind in their beds to trick the enemy.

Spy shadow

This spy leaves a dummy propped up in his window, so that it can be seen from outside.

The enemy soon gets tired of watching and falls asleep. The spy then slips away, unwatched.

Who's watching who?

Who is this mysterious person behind the fence who goes on watching hour after hour?

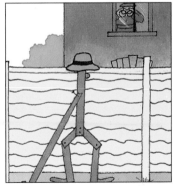

Trapped inside his house, this spy thinks he is being watched. He can't go out on his mission.

Laying a trail

You might need to show a contact where you
have gone. Here are some signs you can use
to lay a trail. Make them with twigs, stones
or deep scratches in the ground.

Trail signs

Make your signs just big enough for a
careful observer to see them. Put them
at the side of your path so they will not be
disturbed by other walkers. Make sure you
are not being watched when you lay the trail.

Go straight ahead   **Not this way**   **End of trail**

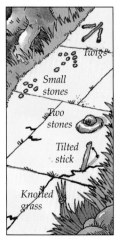

Twigs

Small stones

Two stones

Tilted stick

Knotted grass

Twigs

Broken twigs

Row of stones

Small stones

Crossed twigs

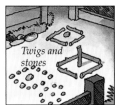

Twigs and stones

Caution

Twigs

Stones

Turn left (or right)

Twigs

Small stones

Broken twig

Big stone with a small one on the left.

Tilted stick at 45°

Also use these signs for turning right – just point them the opposite way.

Indian signs

When you are laying a trail, you can use these signs for messages. Chalk them on stones or scratch them on dry earth. They are based on the picture writing used by Sioux Indians, who scratched messages on dried animal skins and tree bark.

Time of day

Morning Noon Evening Day Night

Weather and landscape

Grass Road Rain Sun

Lake River Sea Tree Forest

Camp
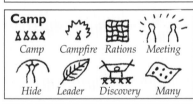
Camp Campfire Rations Meeting

Hide Leader Discovery Many

War

Fight Prisoner Enemy Defeated enemy

People
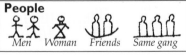
Men Woman Friends Same gang

Actions
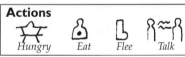
Hungry Eat Flee Talk

Useful signs
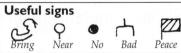
Bring Near No Bad Peace

Spy message test

These messages were left for you by your contact. Can you figure out what they mean? Use your imagination and some guess work*. The answers are on page 32.

1

2

3

4

5

6

*Clue: The symbols show ideas, rather than single words. Think of the meaning of the whole message.

Disguises

Good spies wear disguises so they will not be recognized by the enemy. They can then watch them without being discovered. You can keep enemy spies guessing by changing your disguises.

Tips for disguising

When on a mission, you need to move around unrecognized. Here are some ideas to help you.

Even when you're in disguise, avoid being photographed. Then enemies won't have a record of your features.

Choose clothes that help you fit into your surroundings.

Beware of dogs that know you. They will recognize your smell.

Try to change your disguise as often as you can. The watching enemy will be confused and will easily lose track of you.

A good way to baffle the enemy spies is to wear the same sort of clothing as the local people. You will blend in completely.

Look at me

You can help a friend to spy by creating a diversion. This distracts the enemy's attention.

Double disguise

To trick the enemy, you and your friend dress the same. Hide your faces as you pass an enemy spy.

When you have passed by, he will follow. Separate and he will not know which one to follow.

Thinking up new disguises

When you need a new disguise, try watching other people to see how they behave. Do it carefully. Most people don't like being stared at and remember that they may be enemy spies.

For instance, people eat differently. Some hold their knives and forks carefully and eat slowly. Others eat fast and spill things.

Watch people sleep. Some open their mouths and snore. Others' heads fall forward.

How do people sit? Some cross their legs and others waggle their feet.

Quick cover-ups

Disguises don't have to be elaborate or take a long time to create. Here are some ideas for quick disguises.

Hiding your face

Whether or not you are in disguise, it is a good idea to keep your face hidden. This makes it very difficult for enemy spies to remember and recognize you.

Always carry a handkerchief in your pocket. In an emergency, whip it out, as if to use it.

Pretend to drop some money. Make sure that the enemy spy doesn't stop to help you!

Use an umbrella to hide your face in moments of danger.

Carry a bag and bend right over to look inside.

Telephone voices

Here's how to disguise your voice over the telephone.

Try to speak while holding a pencil in your teeth.

Purse your lips as though you were going to whistle.

Try to speak when smiling very wide or when frowning.

Try holding your nose when speaking.

Change your walk

A good spy knows that people can be recognized by their walks. You can change your walk to fit the disguise you are wearing. Try some of these.

Wear high-heeled shoes and totter along, taking small steps as you go.

Turn your toes in. This will make you move in a really different way.

Walk quickly taking very big strides. Swing your arms and put your heels down firmly.

Bend sideways and hold your hand on your hip as if you have a bad back. Walk slowly.

Quick disguise collection

A good spy needs lots of clothes and shoes. Different bags, hats, gloves, belts, scarves, umbrellas, glasses and cheap earrings and necklaces are also useful. Collect as many kinds as you can and keep them in your secret disguise wardrobe.

Special effects

To become a real master of disguise, good spies have to be able to change their appearances dramatically. Try these ideas.

Face make-up

Draw on different shaped lips with a shade of lipstick that contrasts with your skin.

Brush pale blue eye shadow around your eyes to make your face appear tired and pale.

Bandage

Fake a head injury. Take a bandage or a long strip of white material. Start with it rolled up.

Bind it as tightly as you can, then it won't slip. Fasten the end with a safety pin.

Black teeth

Cut out small squares of gummed black paper and stick them to your teeth.

Eye patch

Cut out a round piece of cardboard. Paint it black. Make holes and tie it on with elastic.

Looking fat

One of the best ways to disguise yourself is to change your shape completely. Try making yourself look fatter than you really are.

You can make your stomach look big by tying one or two cushions around your waist. Wrap a small towel around your shoulders to make them broad. Tie scarves around your legs and arms and wear big clothes over the top. Put on big gloves and shoes.

Looking old

People's appearances change as they grow older. For a brilliant disguise, make yourself look like an old person.

Old people are often a little unsteady, so move slowly. Hold onto things to steady yourself.

Old people often stoop a little. This makes them seem shorter. You could use a walking stick.

Pretend to be very stiff. Bending down slowly is a good way to have a look around.

Sitting down for ages and knitting is a good excuse for watching and waiting.

27

Detecting disguises

However good you are at disguising yourself, it is just as important to be able to recognize when someone else is in disguise. Here are some ways to get good at detecting disguises.

Spy spotting

Go out on an observation trip. Take a notebook and pen to record what you see.

Notice how people look. With practice, you will soon realize when someone is in disguise.

Hair, hats and glasses

Remember that hair, hats and glasses change the appearance of people's faces dramatically.

Above is someone wearing different disguises. Would you guess he was the same man?

28

False beard trick

To get a close look at a suspicious-looking beard, pretend you can see an insect caught in it.

Smudge test

Offer to rub a smudge off someone's face with your handkerchief if you think they may be wearing make-up.

These clumsy waitresses may be spies in disguise.

Suspicious workers

Watch people at work to see if they are used to doing their jobs. If they look awkward, they might be enemy spies in disguise. For instance, these waiters on the left might not be real ones!

Spy identity test

Remember to check people's appearances from behind. Back views can be difficult to disguise. For instance, look at the two people on the right. Which do you think is the woman? Find the answer on page 32.

More spy tests

Here are some more tricky spy tests to challenge your spying skills. There are some clues in the box at the bottom of this page. The answers to these and the other spy tests in the book are on page 32.

Spy disguise test

A good spy may be sent on a secret mission at any time, to anywhere in the world. Spies must wear the right clothes so that they will not be noticed. Below is a spy's wardrobe for keeping hats. Which hat or headdress would you choose for these six different countries?

Clues

- *Spy disguise test*
  Knowing the countries might help: 1 is Russia; 2 is Scotland; 3 is the United States; 4 is Mexico; 5 is Egypt; 6 is Switzerland.
- *Spy escape test*
  Apart from using a code, how else can you make writing secret? See page 12.
- *Spy spotting test*
  Look for hidden people, as well as the obvious ones in the crowd.

Spy escape test

You have been captured and imprisoned by the enemy. You have no weapons or spy equipment – only what is shown on the right.

Your captors have allowed you to write one letter, but you know it must not look suspicious. They can crack even the hardest code. How do you use this letter to send a message to your spy ring asking for help?*

Spy spotting test

The Embassy has invited many special guests to a reception. Presidents and important people from many foreign countries are there. Your HQ has been tipped off that enemy spies are disguised and will attend the reception to gather secret information.

How many suspicious-looking people can you see?

Hint: "Mother" is the code name for your spy chief.

Spy language

Contact - a member of your spy ring, who you meet by arrangement.

Cover - part of the landscape that is useful for hiding behind.

Dead - "Victor is dead" means that Victor has been caught by the enemy.

Drop - hiding place for secret messages.

HQ - headquarters, or the building where the spy ring's operations are directed from.

Mailbox - person who holds a message for a spy.

Master spy - head of a spy ring.

Plain message- an uncoded message.

Quarry - a person who is being followed.

Rendezvous - a place where you arrange to meet your contact.

Spy ring - a group of spies who work together.

Suspect - someone who may be an enemy spy.

Tail - someone who is following another person.

Answers to spy tests

Spy message test (page 21)

1. Hide in the forest near the river.
2. No night meeting.
3. Bring rations to campfire in the evening.
4. Meeting in the morning by the lake.
5. Leader of the enemy talks about peace.
6. Men have discovered our camp – flee.

Spy identity test (page 29)

The figure on the right is a woman and the figure on the left is a man. Look at the sizes of the two figures, not just their clothes.

Spy disguise test (page 30)

1. A Russian fur hat.
2. A Scottish tartan cap.
3. An American cowboy hat.
4. A Mexican straw hat.
5. An Arab headdress.
6. A woolly ski hat.

Spy escape test (page 31)

Write an ordinary letter as if you were really sending it to your mother, but address the envelope to your secret HQ. Sharpen the matchstick against the prison wall. You then have three options. Using the matchstick you can either write a secret message on the letter in spit or juice from the apple core. Alternatively, you can blow the candle out and make a wax pencil to write with. Don't forget to use an indicator to show the chief spy which method you have used. The chief can then organize your escape.

Spy spotting test (page 31)

There are at least 20 suspicious-looking people at the Embassy reception. Did you spot them all?

This book is based on material previously published in *The Usborne Spy's Guidebook*.

First published in 1996 by Usborne Publishing Ltd, Usborne House, 83-85 Saffron Hill, London EC1N 8RT, England.
Copyright © 1996, 1978 Usborne Publishing Ltd.
The name Usborne and the device 🐝 are Trade Marks of Usborne Publishing Ltd.
First published in America August 1996 UE
Printed in Italy.